HORSEFLY

by **Alice Hoffman**

Paintings by **Steve Johnson** and **Lou Fancher**

Hyperion Books for Children ¤ New York

1 3 5 7 9 10 8 6 4 2

Printed in Hong Kong

Library of Congress Cataloging-in-Publication Data

Hoffman, Alice.

Horsefly / Alice Hoffman ; illustrations by Steve Johnson and Lou Fancher.

p.   cm.

Summary: Jewel is afraid of everything until her grandfather gives her

a special horse to raise, a small horse with the ability to fly.

ISBN 0-7868-0367-3 (trade ed.) — ISBN 0-7868-2318-6 (lib. bdg.)

[1. Horses—Fiction. 2. Fear—Fiction. 3. Grandfathers—Fiction.] I. Johnson, Steve, 1960– ill.

II. Fancher, Lou, ill. III. Title.

PZ7.H67445 Ho 2000   99-86583

Visit www.hyperionchildrensbooks.com

To Wolfe and to Jake
and to my friends who love horses

A.H.

To Cassie, who loves books

S.J. & L.F.

On the edge of a prairie so wide it was called the sea of grass was a town where everyone loved horses. As soon as a stranger walked into town, he could smell horses and the sweet scent of hay. At night, babies in their cribs fell asleep to the sound of horses snoring out in the corrals, and in the morning they woke to the rolling echo of horses running free in the pastures.

People here were worth the sum of their horses—how many you owned meant more than how much money you had in the bank. The richest man in town was Florian Taylor, who owned Cloud Ranch, where he kept forty white horses, the finest in town.

When you looked up at Cloud Ranch on a clear day, those horses did look exactly like clouds. When they all ran together, the ground began to tremble and Florian Taylor's granddaughter, Jewel, hid under her bed. She covered her ears with her hands, in the hopes that those horses would disappear into thin air, just the way clouds sometimes do.

Jewel was afraid of everything. She hated thunder and lightning, and was equally terrified of mice and mountain lions. Even though she lived at Cloud Ranch, the one thing she swore she would never do, no matter what, was ride a horse. Florian Taylor tried everything to convince her otherwise. He bought her a pair of beautiful red boots and a cowgirl hat. He tried to explain what it felt like to gallop across the sea of grass at twilight, when the doves were flying close to the fields and the earth seemed endless.

Jewel always listened politely, but she would not change her mind. She tossed her red boots into the very back of her closet and stuffed the cowgirl hat into a kitchen cabinet.

And then one rainy night, Florian Taylor knocked on his granddaughter's bedroom door. It was a little after midnight, but Jewel was not asleep. She had been frightened by the way her curtain was blowing in the breeze and by the beat of the rain against the roof, and so she was hiding under her bed.

But when her grandfather called for her to hurry, she did, grabbing a sweater to pull over her nightgown. She followed Florian out of the house, led by a pool of yellow lantern light. They ran through the rain to the stable where forty horses were sleeping. Jewel could almost hear her heart pounding.

They passed by Snowbird's stall. Snowbird was the proudest of Florian's horses. This mare was spoiled and bad-tempered, and no one but Florian dared to ride her. But Snowbird was not who they had come to visit; it was the foal she had just given birth to. Florian hung the lantern on a wooden peg so Jewel could see. There, in a pile of fresh hay, was the tiniest foal in the world. Why, it looked more like a puppy than a pony. Unlike every other horse at Cloud Ranch, this one wasn't white. He was a deep chestnut brown with a black mane and tail. He was so silly-looking, and so very small, that for a moment Jewel forgot he was a horse, and she laughed out loud.

"That's the way Snowbird feels," Florian said. "He's too scrawny and little to be a real horse. She won't take care of him. Matter of fact, she tried to squash him like a bug."

The foal shook his head and whinnied. In spite of his size, he was a horse, all right, and Jewel felt uneasy. She might have turned and run right then, if her grandfather hadn't handed her a bottle of mare's milk sweetened with sugar.

"He's yours now," Florian Taylor called over his shoulder. His black raincoat swirled out behind him as he left Jewel alone in the barn.

Jewel stood there for a long time, too frightened to move. At last, she went into the stall and fed the foal his bottle. He really was cute, if you liked horses, if the very sight of them didn't make you shiver with fear.

When the foal finished his bottle, he was drowsy. Jewel tiptoed out of the stall, took the lantern down from the peg, then headed back to the house. The sky was still inky and dawn was an hour away. Jewel thought she was finally free of the foal, but halfway to the house she heard something behind her. It was the *clip-clop* of little hooves.

Jewel began to run, and the *clip-clop*ping went faster, too.

She dashed up the porch steps and raced inside with the *clip-clop*ping still following her right through the hallway and into her room. Finally, Jewel got into her bed and hid under the covers, but the little horse just stood there, breathing softly, smelling of hay.

"Go away," Jewel whispered, but he wouldn't. Instead, the foal slept curled up on her rug.

In the morning, Florian didn't even blink when Jewel came in for breakfast with the foal trailing behind. After that, the little horse was like a member of the family.

Jewel called him Bug, and she quickly got used to the way he followed her around. When the cook, Marie, asked why Jewel was afraid of the other horses but had no fear of Bug, Jewel laughed. "He's not exactly a horse," she said.

"He eats like one," Marie said. "He runs like one. He stinks like one."

"He's not like the others," Jewel said.

By the end of the summer, Bug was as big as a Saint Bernard—too small to stay with the horses, too large to be a house pet. Jewel kept him tied to the front porch to make sure he didn't get into trouble. But one day Jewel didn't tie the rope tightly enough, and Bug followed her to school.

"It's a mule," someone cried.

"No, it's a donkey." A girl laughed.

"Hey, what do you call this thing?" one of the boys shouted as Jewel went to lead Bug away. "It sure isn't a horse."

"He's better than yours," Jewel heard herself say.

"Prove it," the boy said.

Jewel had never been on a horse, but now she pulled herself up on Bug's back. Even though Jewel was small, her feet almost touched the ground.

On the count of three the horses took off. Jewel was so scared, she closed her eyes. She didn't notice that the boy had suddenly pulled back on his horse's reins. "Turn left!" the boy shouted to Jewel. "Slow him down!"

When Jewel opened her eyes, she saw they were racing straight toward a cliff. She tried to hold Bug back, but it was too late. Jewel had no choice: she jumped off. There was nothing to do but watch as Bug ran over the cliff.

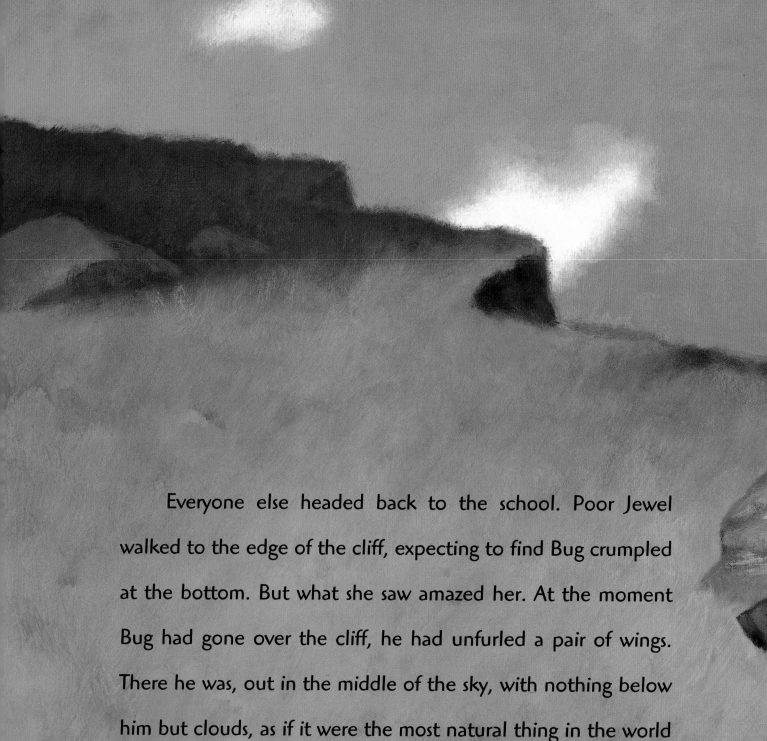

Everyone else headed back to the school. Poor Jewel
walked to the edge of the cliff, expecting to find Bug crumpled
at the bottom. But what she saw amazed her. At the moment
Bug had gone over the cliff, he had unfurled a pair of wings.
There he was, out in the middle of the sky, with nothing below
him but clouds, as if it were the most natural thing in the world
for a pony to be flying through the air.

At first, Jewel was afraid to ride him—or was it fly him? She never could tell. They started out slowly, a foot above the ground, then two, then higher. Jewel held on tight, but after a while she grew braver. She dared a loop-the-loop, then a sky-circle, then a dive-bomb. On earth, Jewel was still her same nervous self, but in the sky she was fearless.

She wished she could describe to her grandfather how it felt
to fly above the sea of grass. She longed to tell him how a cloud
tasted, how the wind whispered, but she didn't dare. She kept the
secret of the flying horse, and it seemed no one would ever find
out. Bug's wings, after all, were like those of a bat's, and completely
hidden when folded.

Jewel became so comfortable up in the air that she often fell asleep while Bug grazed among the treetops. She must have been sleeping the day they were spotted. A thin man in a black suit was standing beside his van, changing a flat tire on his way from here to there. This man, whose name was Morrison, was the ringmaster of a circus, and he never stayed in one place for long.

Every evening, Morrison boldly announced acts that would amaze and astound. But now it was Morrison's mouth that dropped open. There above him was a flying horse. A pair of wings that could make a smart man rich.

That night, Morrison and the circus strong man sneaked onto Cloud Ranch. Before you could count to three they had Bug tied up in their van and had headed toward the far side of town. Somehow Jewel knew. She ran to her window to see that Bug was no longer tied to the porch. Jewel grabbed her jacket and went out into the starless night. The ground was wet, so she could see the tire tracks from the circus van. She followed the trail away from Cloud Ranch, to the abandoned field where the circus had set up.

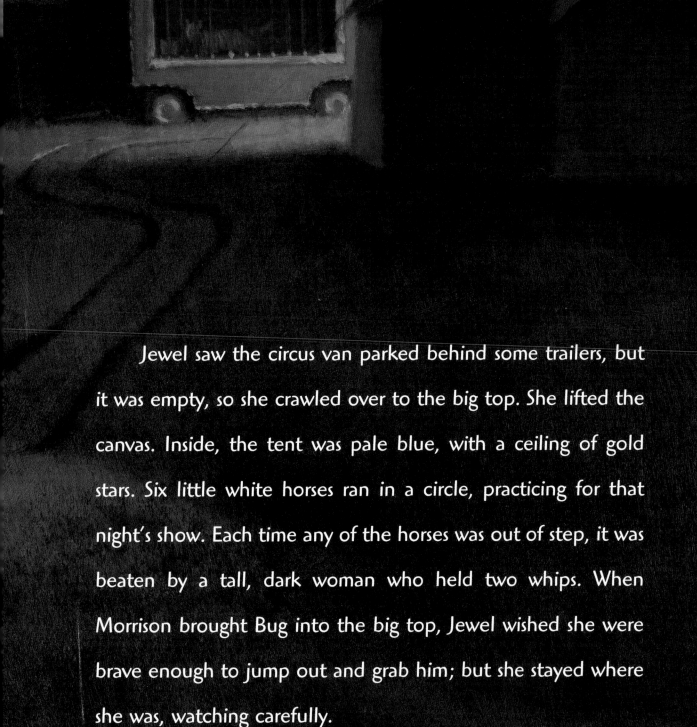

Jewel saw the circus van parked behind some trailers, but it was empty, so she crawled over to the big top. She lifted the canvas. Inside, the tent was pale blue, with a ceiling of gold stars. Six little white horses ran in a circle, practicing for that night's show. Each time any of the horses was out of step, it was beaten by a tall, dark woman who held two whips. When Morrison brought Bug into the big top, Jewel wished she were brave enough to jump out and grab him; but she stayed where she was, watching carefully.

"What is this supposed to be?" the woman in charge of the horses asked. Poor Bug was tied up in ropes. "What an ugly, filthy creature."

"Take a look." Morrison cut one of the ropes and lifted one of Bug's wings. "This filthy creature's going to make us rich."

Nearby, a tiger paced in its cage. But Jewel didn't have time to be frightened. Not if she wanted to rescue Bug. First, she needed to disguise herself. In a big, old trunk she found a costume that fit perfectly. When she looked at herself in the mirror, she was delighted to see a real circus girl looking back.

That night, everyone from town came to see the show, but no one recognized Jewel. The air smelled of popcorn and cotton candy and horses. When Morrison shouted for the show to begin, the woman who was so cruel came racing in, lashing at Bug and the six white horses with her whip.

As soon as Bug saw Jewel, he reared on his hind legs and was lashed three more times.

"You foolish little pony!" the cruel woman screamed. "I'll make you behave!"

Jewel could wait no longer. She ran into the ring and jumped onto Bug's back. In her circus costume she looked like part of the act, and everyone applauded. Even those children who had teased her before whistled and stomped their feet.

"Get out of here!" the woman who was so mean to horses demanded, which is exactly what Jewel planned to do.

Jewel leaned down and whispered to Bug, and immediately he unfurled his wings. The crowd gasped when his hooves lifted off the ground. Higher and higher Bug flew, up to the ceiling of stars.

"Catch them!" cried Morrison, but it was too late for that. Bug and Jewel would have flown right through the top of the tent, had Jewel not looked down to see the six tiny horses, all huddled together in the ring. They were the saddest-looking creatures she had ever seen.

Bug and Jewel suddenly swooped down. People ran this way and that. Bug and Jewel dive-bombed, knocking off Morrison's hat, grabbing the cruel horse trainer's whips and breaking them in half.

"This way!" Jewel shouted. "Follow us!"

When Bug flew through the door of the tent, the circus horses raced out after him. They ran through the town, into the sea of grass. Jewel and Bug kept pace from above, beneath the stars, cutting across the inky-blue night, the wind singing in their ears.

That night the six little white horses slept in the stable next to Snowbird, who was quite amazed to discover they could dance on their hind legs and climb on one another's backs, building a tower that allowed the littlest horse to pour out the extra buckets of grain that hung above the stalls.

In the morning, Florian Taylor found Jewel out on the front porch, having breakfast with Bug. She was wearing the red boots she had kept at the back of her closet. She had taken out the cowgirl hat and discovered it fit her perfectly.

"Those look real good on you," Florian told his granddaughter.

Jewel smiled. She led her grandfather out to the sea of grass and showed him what it was like to ride across the sky. Not that Florian was surprised. He had known exactly what he was giving Jewel on that rainy night when the little horse with wings had been born.

Now and then, on clear blue days, a shadow falls across the prairie. People in town gaze upward. They stop, knee-deep in the sea of grass, and lift a hand to shade their eyes. For a minute or two they might think they spy something, up in the sky.

"A great day for flying," Florian Taylor always says to his neighbors on days like this, and no one has disagreed with him yet.